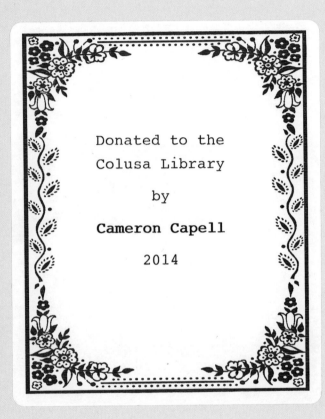

Donated to the
Colusa Library

by

Cameron Capell

2014

Presented to

....

From

....

Just Like Jesus Said

SECRETLY DO
Good Deeds

Illustrations by Susan Reagan

Melody Carlson

Broadman & Holman Publishers Nashville, Tennessee

Text copyright ©2002 by Melody Carlson
Illustration copyright ©2002 by Susan Reagan
Cover and interior design: UDG | DesignWorks

Published in 2002 by Broadman & Holman Publishers,
Nashville, Tennessee

LIBRARY OF CONGRESS CATALOGING-IN-PUBLICATION DATA

Carlson, Melody.
Secretly do good deeds / by Melody Carlson ; illustrations by Susan Reagan.
p. cm. -- (Just like Jesus said series)
ISBN 0-8054-2384-2
[1. Conduct of life--Fiction. 2. Christian life--Fiction. 3. Stories in rhyme.]
I. Reagan, Susan, ill. II. Title.

PZ8.3.C19475 Do 2002
[E]--dc21   2001043315

All rights reserved. Printed in Korea.

ISBN 0-8054-2384-2

2 3 4 5 6 07 06 05 04 03

Secretly Do Good Deeds

ONE REALLY WEIRD DAY, something happened to me,

Somebody did something that I couldn't see.

It wasn't a bad thing — no, not at all.

And it wasn't a big thing — no, it was quite small.

And yet it was something I'll never forget.

Something so special, so thoughtful and yet

The person who did this has never be found.

They managed to do it when I wasn't around.

I'll bet you now wonder what happened to me,

Who did this great something that I couldn't see?

And yet if I told you, you'd just shrug and say,

"Well, that could've happened on any old day."

And so I must tell you how it changed my heart.

And after it happened, is when I did start

To do *secret somethings* — to make people smile.

I think, and I plan; it can take quite a while.

But first let me tell you 'bout my friend, Marie,

She was just as messy as messy could be.

Her room was a wreck — not a thing could be found.

So I sneaked right on over — she wasn't around.

I talked to her mom and she promised to keep,

My surprise as a secret — she'd breathe not a peep.

I cleaned and I straightened the room neat and nice.

And Marie was so happy at her big surprise!

And then for my mommy,

when she was upstairs,

I dusted the shelves and the

tables and chairs.

I never did tell her, but, boy,

did I grin.

And when she's not looking,

I'll do it again!

Then when my Grandma

was busily cooking,

I went right outside

when she wasn't looking.

I swept her whole porch,

the best that I could,

And when I got done,

I sure did feel good!

15

But one of the best secret things that I've done,

Was one of those things that was just the best fun!

It happened one Sunday before Sunday school,

I did it for Tommy, and it was so cool!

When offering is taken (it happens each time)

Poor Tommy feels badly, he hasn't a dime.

But this time I slipped my own coins in his pocket

And boy, did he smile when *he* got to drop it!

Then there was the time

when I saw Aunt Louise;

I knew just the thing I could do

that would please.

I slipped a small note in her purse

that said:

"I love you so much,"

was how my note read.

19

And there was the time

when I saw Miss McFarden,

And I pulled the weeds from

out of her garden.

She never did see me —

or never said so.

But then how her flowers did

grow and grow!

And there are those times when I walk on tip-toes,

To see Baby Jenny, and tickle her little nose.

I coo and I grin and I make funny faces.

Between her crib bars, between those small spaces.

And it makes me laugh when I see her smile,

And sometimes I stay and we talk for awhile.

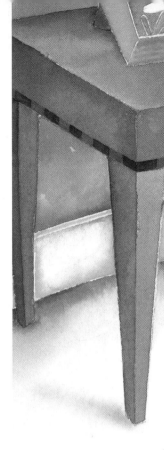

But please do not think that

I'm always good,

Or always do everything

just like I should.

For I get in trouble —

make mistakes like you do.

To say I was perfect just

wouldn't be true.

For
Kitty

But one thing I've found that

makes me feel right

Is something done well,

but just out of sight.

To make someone happy,

makes my heart just glow,

But it's oh so much better,

when they do not know.

Like when I found Daddy

all tired and dry,

And I put a glass of cold water nearby.

I watched as he drank it

then looked all around.

But I was well hidden,

and couldn't be found!

And I guess the reason I love this so much,

Is that it's just like a big hug or a touch.

Except that they never quite know that it's me.

And that makes me happy, as happy can be.

And now I will share my fun secret with you.

It's something Lord Jesus said that we should do.

"Do your good deeds when no one can see,

And God will reward you eternally!"

"But when you give to the needy,
do not let your left hand know what your
right hand is doing, so that your
giving may be in secret. Then your Father,
who sees what is done in secret,
will reward you."

MATTHEW 6:3–4